I0623617

Cogs and Daggers: The Adventures of Ivy and Selena Book 1

Cogs and Daggers, Volume 1

JM Steiner

Published by LPS Publishing House LLC, 2024.

COGS AND DAGGERS: THE ADVENTURES OF IVY AND SELENA BOOK 1

First edition. March 6, 2024.

Copyright © 2024 JM Steiner.

ISBN: 978-1956376364

Written by JM Steiner.

JM STEINER

COGS AND DAGGERS

THE ADVENTURES OF IVY AND SELENA
BOOK 1

Cogs and Daggers
The Adventures of Ivy and Selena
Book 1

By JM Steiner

Chapter One

Not a lot of people understood what it meant to be shunned by society, but Selena did.

After all, if she didn't understand it, she wouldn't be chasing a rat down the streets of her city for a piece of equipment.

"Get back here!" Selena screamed before realizing, perhaps a bit too late, that the rat she was chasing had no inkling of listening to a word that she said.

The streets of Hickory were bustling, just as they always were. Selena had to bob and weave between shoppers, children playing, and police who were walking the streets with their eyes peeled for trouble. Normally, Selena would be more worried about running around chasing an animal and getting in everyone's way, but Selena was used to blending in.

That was essential to her survival.

Cars floated overhead, honking their horns at the other cars who weren't moving. Gangs of teenagers who were stuck to the ground listened to angry music, bobbing their heads up and down to try to look cool. A man with a cybernetic leg walked by, forcing everyone to get out of his way.

Selena's heart ached for the man as he hobbled down the packed street looking for money or anyone who could help him. Not one helping hand reached out to him, and it was all because of a cybernetic leg. As if losing a limb was somehow contagious.

Selena would have helped him if she could, but with her current situation, she was clearly a bit busy.

The rat dove under a vendor's table, causing Selena to lightly shove someone out of her way to continue on the path. They screamed vulgarities at her, and Selena shouted back a half assed apology. She would be forgotten in the next ten minutes.

The rat was losing speed, and so was Selena. Her heart was racing, and she could feel the sweat dripping down her brow. Her legs felt like they were on fire, and she was so close to giving up just so she could breathe that she wasn't sure where to go from there.

But then, the rat made a mistake.

As more and more people got closer to the rat, running towards Hickory Market, the rodent began to panic. It took a sharp right turn and ran straight toward what Selena knew from experience to be a dead end. She smirked and pushed herself forward.

The rat came to a screeching halt when it realized there was a giant wall hovering in front of him, and no nooks and crannies for him to hide in. He was about to turn and run the other way when Selena put all her energy into jumping on the rat.

When her hands caught on to the rat, she squeezed so tight that she would have been shocked if she hadn't choked the poor thing to death.

"Ha!" she cheered. "Caught you!"

The rat only squealed in response.

Selena pried the piece the rat stole from his hands and exhaled with relief. She needed this piece to help construct the finishing touches on one of her biggest projects to date. The client was important, to say the least, and if they didn't get what they wanted, Selena would face serious consequences.

She dropped the rat gently, despite the fact that it made a point to run out and about with her piece. Then, she pocketed the piece and turned around.

She wasn't looking where she was going - and it was one of the only reasons why she ran straight into a man that was twice her size.

"Well, hello there," The voice boomed over her. "What did I stumble into here?"

Selena felt like a deer caught in the headlights. Her entire body was frozen in place as she heard the heavy breathing that came with an older man. Selena shivered and took a step back, putting distance between herself and the new creepy man.

"I'm sorry," Selena apologized. "I didn't mean to run into you like that. I wasn't watching where I was going."

"Well, I was," The man purred. "I saw what you put in your pocket. That would cost a pretty penny on the black market."

"It's mine," Selena tried to stay strong and drop her voice lower. "I made it myself. You can't have it."

The man laughed, deeply and mischievously. There was a hint of malice in the way that his body shook and his eyes narrowed. When he smiled at her, she could see that he was missing a few teeth.

"I don't give a rat's ass who made the piece, sweetie. I want it. Hell, I want more than that."

Two other men emerged from the shadows. Selena had the deepest rage against the dumb rat that ran this way, pinning her against the wall and giving her no way to run. She shrunk back, trying to make herself look as small as possible.

"The way I see it, you have about two options," He began to explain. "You can give me that piece you made, and you can be on your way. Or, you can pay the three of us back for not stealing it from you some other way. Like I said," He looked her up and down with prying eyes.

"That piece is worth a pretty penny."

Selena knew how much the piece was worth because she made it. She also knew damn good and well that she wasn't giving it up for anything. It was more than just something that she made.

She needed to keep it for someone else.

"I'll scream," She snapped. "I'll scream so loud that people will hear you and come running."

"Oh, will they?" The man laughed. "You're just a lone girl in a back alley surrounded by a group of men. Who's going to believe that we did anything to you? You're the one who's here with us, you know."

Selena swallowed.

"They'll believe me," She bluffed. "They will!"

The truth was, Selena didn't know who they would believe. She was just a piece of lower-class trash to them. Who cared what she said or who she said it to? Who cared if she was being attacked on the streets when someone else said that she started it, or worse, that she wanted it? She clutched the item in her hand so tightly that she could feel it prickling her skin, drawing blood. Was this stupid little piece of equipment worth losing everything that she held dear?

She didn't even have to hesitate.

Of course it was.

"You think they'll believe you?" The man laughed, spitting up saliva as he did. "Really? You?"

Selena felt her anger boiling up within her. She normally didn't like telling people off, but there was just something about this guy that really grinded her gears. Was it the fact that he was implying something worse than death as a threat to get her to leave them alone? Maybe. But what Selena figured was the thing that pissed her off the most was simple.

He was a hypocrite.

"What makes you think that they'll believe you either?" She cried. "You're just a stupid, spindly lower class like me, right? What makes you think they'll care about either of us?!"

"Exactly," He smirked and leaned closer.

"No one will come to help you."

His hand reached for Selena's object.

She could feel her heartbeat racing in her ears. She knew it was coming and she still hated the realization that someone was grabbing at her, reaching for something that was hers and not theirs. They were trying to take it away.

Selena ducked, avoiding his reaching for her. She wasn't a fighter, surely, but she also wasn't a pansy. She would defend herself - and all the things that mattered to her. She reached down towards her ankle and pulled out her switchblade, flicking it open from the ground where she had ducked down at. She heard the man above her cry out in surprise before she sliced at his leg, hard and deep.

He screamed and reached for his wound, falling over. Selena jumped up then, knowing she had to fight but also wanting so badly to run. She was holding her blade tightly, and she wasn't sure who to swing at next if the other two came forward.

"You little bitch!" One of the men screamed. He charged at Selena, but she didn't care.

She tucked and rolled on the ground to dodge them, reminding herself of a pillbug. When she got back up on her feet, though, the men were already on her. One of them grabbed her by the hair and yanked her, hard, away from the others. In the chaos, she dropped her switchblade. She screamed as loud as she could, but the second man slapped his hand over her mouth and held it there, despite her struggling.

"Where's the item?" He snarled. "Where. Is. It?"

Selena glared at him. Part of her found it to be pretty hilarious when she realized that even if she knew where the item was, she couldn't tell him where it was. He had his hand over her mouth.

His eyes began to wander, though. He stared at Selena's chest, at her legs. When the sick smile spread over his cheeks, Selena made sure to send her foot as hard and as fast as she could towards his face.

When her foot connected, he screamed and stumbled backwards. Blood began to drip down his chin, and his eyes became enraged. Selena knew that there was no way she could win in this situation - The grip in her hair from the man from behind her was a not-so-subtle reminder. But, by God, she was going to make them fight for it.

She was going to make them pay.

She prepped her legs to do more kicking and her mouth to do more screaming when she heard the sounds of someone running on the roof.

Selena blinked.

Running on the *roof*?

Selena looked up, and so did the three men who captured her. Then, from the roof, a shadow leapt down and landed square on the chin of the man covering Selena's mouth.

The shadow landed with it's foot on the captors chest, and it took Selena a moment to realize exactly who it was. When she figured it out, Selena smirked.

All of these guys were dead.

Before anyone else could react, a whizzing sound rushed through the air. Then, a knife, small but equally as dangerous, landed square in the eye of the first man.

He fell to the ground, wailing like a child. His leg was still bleeding, though Selena doubted that was the most important thing in his mind right now. He was probably going to pass out soon from the pain.

The one holding Selena's hair dropped her and took off running. Selena was going to call out, but it didn't matter. The shadow threw some bolas spinning in the air until they wrapped around the ankles of the fleeing man and caused him to come crashing down onto the ground.

He screamed and got a mouth full of dirt.

Selena scrambled to her feet and got the dagger, still holding tightly to the object in her other hand. She refused to drop it, even in the chaos. She stood next to the shadow, looking down on the pig of a man.

"Ivy," she whispered. "Need some help?"

Selena's sister smirked and looked up, rolling her neck. "Nah. I've got this."

"It's a bit early for you to be on the prowl," Selena snickered.

"Never too early to go after my kid sister who thought it would be a great idea to chase a rat through town square," Ivy snarled.

Selena rubbed the back of her neck. "Sorry."

Ivy rolled her eyes.

"You're so dead," The man threatened. "You're so dead and you don't even know."

"Big talk for the man with his face in the dirt," Ivy snarled. Then, she looked back at Selena.

"Are you sure you're okay?"

"I'm good," Selena nodded honestly. "I got a good cut in there somewhere. Next time, maybe they'll think twice about taking something that doesn't belong to them."

Ivy rolled her eyes. "This isn't an after-school special, Selena."

"If it was an after school special, then it wouldn't be one that was G-Rated," the man coughed. "You pissed off the wrong people."

Ivy laughed. "No, I think *you* pissed off the wrong people."

She finally stepped off of him, and the man got on his feet with rage painted all over his face. His chest was heaving in and out, and it felt like maybe he was boiling. The entire expression that he was offering almost wanted to make Selena laugh. She understood that this was a dire situation, but the man just looked like a red potato.

"I didn't do anything of that sort," the man growled.

He reached over and yanked down his shirt sleeve, revealing some kind of tattoo. Of course, Selena and Ivy just blinked at it. They had genuinely no idea who the ink was representing, and they couldn't care less. The sisters looked at each other from the sides of their eyes and snickered.

"You dare laugh in the face of a Pirate!?" the man screamed. "I should have your tongue for that!"

Ivy moved in a flash. In fact, it was so fast that Selena wondered if she imagined what happened. She had no idea what was happening, but before she knew it, Ivy had a shiny silver knife to the man's face. Her eyes were dark, and her stance was steady.

The man was clearly not prepared to see that.

"I don't think you understood my threat properly," Ivy slowly lowered the silver blade.

The man gasped, and slowly blood began to emerge from his face and pool onto his cheeks. He held his skin together, gasping.

Selena didn't even see Ivy cut him.

"I need you to understand that you may be a Pirate," Ivy wiped the man's blood off on her black pant leg and laughed. "Whatever the hell a Pirate is, anyway."

The man no longer looked angry. He looked terrified.

"But I am a member of the Silver Blades. Clearly, you're unmatched."

"S-S-She's protected by the Silver Blades?!" The man pointed at Selena as she smirked.

"Yes," Ivy answered flatly. "She's quite an important person, actually. If she was harmed in any way, this could mean an open turf war. You understand that, correct?"

He nodded, but he looked terrified. He rolled his neck a little bit, blood continuing to drip down his cheek.

"Yes, I do," he said. "I"m sorry. I didn't know that she was protected."

"Of course you didn't, because whoever these Pirates are clearly haven't had the proper introduction to the world of the undercity," Ivy explained with a sneer.

"But I feel like you and your band of clowns could offer the perfect introduction, no?"

The man nodded and took off in a sprint. He left his friend in the bolas to lie on the ground, begging and crying for help. Ivy glared at the man on the ground and laughed when she made him scream.

"How did you know I was in trouble?" Selena asked as Ivy turned to walk away.

"No thank you for helping me?" she laughed. "No *I love you, sis?*"

Selena glared at Ivy. "You know that's not what's happening here. I just don't know how you knew that I was in danger, or why you're even out at this hour. If the townspeople see you-"

Ivy pulled her hood closer to her face, covering her ivory skin. She flashed her bright green eyes at her sister.

"I got intel that I couldn't ignore," Ivy offered.

Selena needed to know more, but both sisters understood the danger that came with speaking openly in the outside when you were...

Well, them.

Selena and Ivy stepped into a bustling tavern. Men and women talked, laughing and joking, paying the girls no heed. The pair slipped into a back booth where they could talk, undisturbed.

"What intel?" Selena asked. "I know someone didn't tell you that a rat was going to take my piece and run."

Ivy snickered and shook her head. She pulled out a cigarette and lit it, letting the smoke puff out and leaving her to exhale.

"I found out through the chain at... work... that you were going to be double crossed. That's the best and most honest way to put it."

Selena's eyes widened. "By whom?"

Ivy nodded towards the piece of robotics in her hand. Selena felt her blood chill.

"What?" She shook her head. "There's no way that he would do that."

"But he did," Ivy nodded. "My intel was correct. I went to the shop and he arrived with five other men. He planned on taking your invention without paying. I dispatched them quickly, clearly, but since you weren't there, I went to find you."

"Huh," Selena rubbed the back of her neck. "Oddly enough, the rat may have saved me."

"That's certainly one way to think of it," Ivy raised her eyebrows and took another drag of her cigarette. "I told you that you shouldn't have been doing business with the Hog."

Selena sighed. She knew her sister was right.

The Hog was one of the most nefarious underground mob lords, challenged only by the Silver Blades. In fact, they often worked together to conduct their duties. That's how Selena found them in the first place and how she knew that wanted to work with them. She thought they were good people. Well, as good as criminals could be.

"I'm sorry," Ivy sighed. "I know how much this mattered to you."

"I was naive," She sighed. "I should have known better, you know."

"How could you have?" Ivy admitted. "You're... you."

Selena sighed and looked down at the ground. It wasn't fair - she knew it. The life that she and Ivy lived weren't the same, but they were sisters, nonetheless.

In the world that Ivy and Selena were lucky to be born into, the class system was no joke. The shitty thing was it didn't matter about how hard you worked to get from poverty to the top. All that mattered in hindsight was your skin. The color of it, and how... pure it was.

Selena hated to use the word pure, especially after reading the history books to discover exactly what that word used to mean regarding skin color. But now, when the people of Hickory and all over the world talked about the purity of man, they meant the natural body of man.

Which, of course, was free from cybernetic upgrades.

There was a time when cybernetics and cybersecurity were the hot new thing in town. Everyone wanted to upgrade their original human body to something better because that was simply what humans did. Athletes wanted stronger arms, stronger legs. Multi-taskers wanted stronger eyes that would stay open longer and could process multiple tasks at once. Models wanted cybernetic waists that never grew, no matter how much they ate. And of course, for a price, you could get all that and more.

But there was a catch, as there always is when you try to play God.

Sometimes, the machines would glitch. No matter how many times the scientists tried to make sure that the parts of the human body ran smoothly, there was nothing that they could do when it rained or when something happened that unexpectedly shocked the mechanical components. Malfunctions were happening left and right, it seemed, and at first it wasn't that big of a deal.

At first, it was labeled false news. At first, it was seen as stories that were only meant to make people panic when the reality wasn't even a little bit scary. We were told, as people in the real world, that these stories were simply that - just... stories.

Then, on one fateful day that the entire land of Hickory remembers, the malfunction was so great that there wasn't much that anyone could do about it but watch the destruction.

On national TV, one of the President's top secretaries had a cybernetic eye implanted, replacing one of their own human eyes. They were talking to thousands of people on live TV, and before they knew it, their entire head had completely blown up.

Whether or not it was the cybernetics' fault or not wasn't really the issue. The entire world saw those with cybernetics as freaks, as ticking time bombs that could malfunction and blow up at any time. Those who had jumped the gun to immediately get a cybernetic enhancement found themselves struggling for a place in the world where they felt that they fit in, let alone work or a loved one. Quickly, they were cast out on the streets.

It became a struggle for anyone who had cybernetics to even be seen as a person. Men and women who had fought valiantly in World War III or the Great War and lost limbs, only to be replaced by cybernetics, found themselves shunned by the country they had given their lives to defend.

Many people on the internet in forums found it easy to jump on the wagon and blame cybernetics for everything wrong in the lives of commonplace people. Others thought it was interesting that someone's cybernetic would blow up on national television and took to the internet to express their concerns. They were quickly shut down, and it was established among the people that no matter what anyone thought, it was important to remember that there simply was no conspiracy. There was nothing but dysfunctional pieces of metal.

Enter the New Church.

The New Church worshiped nothing outside of the Creator's will for the people. They emerged in the middle of the chaos with the cybernetics, and for years they preached that they were curses brought up from the fires of Hell and given to them to prevent the people of Hickory from entering the gates of Eternal Peace. At first, everyone considered them fanatics. But when the stories started rolling out about the cybernetics' failure, more and more people turned to the church's teaching. Only then did Selena, Ivy, and the rest of Hickory find out what else the church believed and how that would come to ruin the lives of normal people.

Selena and Ivy didn't have any cybernetics, but the beliefs of the church still found a way to harm them. Their lives were spent in hardship, but not because of machinery. The truth was the women weren't normal humans either. No matter how hard they tried, they would never be considered normal humans.

At least, according to the church, they weren't.

The problem with people like Selena and Ivy came down to their skin, eyes, and the fact that they simply couldn't get sick. It wasn't like it was a choice or something - it's just who Selena and Ivy were. "Albinos" was the name that was coined to people like them, whether they wanted it or not. Their pale, icy skin and almost neon eyes seemed to set them apart from every normal human in existence. At first, before the Cybernetic Scandal, Albinos were seen as miracles. The pinnacle human to be tested for cures for cancer and everything in between.

But when the church learned of their existence, they denounced the magic of Albino blood. They were unnatural. Creatures from hell sent to distract the people from the realities of the world.

So, Albinos were cast down with the Cybernetics - Cybers for short. The normal humans with darker skin, normal eyes and all their limbs got to live their lives as normal. But the rest of the people in town? They had no choice. It was dark and grim in the undercity of Hickory. Ivy and Selena had to deal with a lot in their lives, but considering where they ended up, they were lucky.

They were never forced to sell themselves to men or sell parts of themselves to freaks who would give them cybernetics in exchange for money. The girls were as resourceful as they could be, but the truth was that they probably wouldn't have been so lucky if it wasn't for the fact that Selena didn't *look* albino.

Looking Albino was the problem. Ivy certainly looked the part, with her neon green eyes and flashing red hair. To make matters even worse, somehow, Ivy's skin was a pale ivory. It was as white as paper. For whatever reason, Selena's simply wasn't. Her eyes were dark, and her skin reminded everyone around her of a caramel candy. She was still Albino - she'd never once been sick her entire life - but no one judged her for it. No one questioned her about why she was somewhere where Albinos weren't allowed.

At first, Selena hated it. It outed her from the rest of her fellow Albinos and resulted - often - in them hating her. In the early days of being homeless with Ivy, Selena did her best to stay in the shadows and let Ivy do all the talking and interacting with others. Then, Selena realized that she could use her privilege for good. If no one would question her about her skin, and they didn't even blink an eye when it came to the reality of who she was, then she would manipulate them too.

That was how Selena often got away with getting equipment and other pieces for her science projects. She batted her eyelashes and pretended to be a kid who just needed it for their project for school, when in reality that was the farthest thing from the truth.

"I just don't think I understand why he would betray me like that," Selena finally sighed. "I thought we had a good thing going with him."

Ivy pulled her hood in a bit tighter. Selena knew that her sister hated being in places like this, crowded with the Pure Skinned people, but it was better than being out on the street. Ivy would attract too much attention. But, of course, it wasn't like they could hide in the bar for the rest of the night.

"You don't know the unrest that's happening in the underworld, Selena," Ivy shook her head and tapped her fingers against the bar table. "Old gangs are splitting up and new ones are emerging. As we know now, obviously."

Selena snickered. "I doubt they'll last long if they were dumb enough to take you on."

"Well, there's a chance that the idiots really had no idea what they were doing," Ivy smirked and shook her head. "Not everyone who gets into this business is, well, what we would call smart."

Selena understood that all too well. She'd seen many things in her time as her sister's right-hand man, and the cruelty of the undercity was only matched by the idiocy of those who thought they could get away with double crossing mob bosses and other leaders in the undercity.

"Do you think the Hog wants a war with the Silver Blades?" Selena whispered.

Ivy shrugged. "Truthfully, no. I don't think he was thinking when he gave the order. Like I said, the undercity is in shambles right now. I can give him the benefit of the doubt for now, and I imagine he'll appreciate not starting open war with the Silver Blades. Not in this climate, anyway."

Any other day, Selena would assume that the goal of almost any undercity mob lord was to take over other pieces of land for themselves. But now, with this being the fifth time that Ivy had mentioned the undercity being in shambles and facing some kind of terrible endeavor, Selena began to wonder if this was something that she should be concerned with.

"What the hell is even going on in the undercity?" She asked her sister with wide eyes.

Ivy looked around, checking over her shoulder and making sure that no one was looking at the table or listening in. Selena began to wonder in that moment how serious - and moreover, how dangerous - the situation was. If Ivy was concerned with someone listening in on their conversations in a bar with the Pure Skins, this this clearly had reached farther than she anticipated.

"Okay, listen," she whispered. "There have been some... rumors swirling around. Whispers and ideas about someone who found a map that led somewhere pretty awesome."

"What like buried treasure?" Selena whispered back.

"You could say that," Ivy's eyes sparkled with adventure.

Selena blinked, intrigued. "Huh. Tell me more."

"Rumor going around the undercity was simply that the map led to a relic of sorts. Do you remember the time before the Great War?"

Selena shifted uncomfortably. "Not really."

"Good, because neither do I," Ivy smirked.

Selena rolled her eyes but smiled.

"Anyway, this relic was from the time before the Great War. It was directly after WWIII, so it was formed in the second Golden Ages. The rumor said that it was the equivalent to rubbing a modern-day genie bottle, but I'm not that stupid. I have theories that it's the plans for a weapon of mass destruction or something so powerful that whoever finds it will be worshiped just as a way to make sure that they never use it."

"Like a nuke?" Selena's eyes were wide. "I thought that they were tossed away from all facilities when the Great War ended."

"Sure, they were supposed to," Ivy shrugged, "But do you think the American government listens to anyone?"

Selena laughed and then turned it into a cough so nobody looked her way. She didn't want to attract any attention, after all.

"So, I'm assuming that the undercity has everyone who wants their own version of the map?"

"No," Ivy shook her head. "They don't want their own version. They want the original copy, and they plan on stopping at nothing to get it."

"They're searching for the original map?" Selena exhaled. "I thought it was a legend."

"It was," Ivy nodded. "But every good story started as a legend, and they were almost always true. It's worth looking into, don't you think?"

"Wait," Selena shook her head a little. "*You* want to go after this too?!"

Ivy signaled for Selena to shut her trap, or at least lower her voice. Selena did just that.

"I thought you didn't trust any of this!" Selena hissed. "What the hell are you doing endorsing it?"

"Imagine the power that we could have with something that powerful if it did exist, Selena," Ivy hissed. "Just think about it. Seriously. We could fix all of this," Ivy gestured around her. "We could put it back to the way it was before people were 'cybers' and 'Albinos.' We could be *people* again. Don't you get it?"

Selena felt the idea take form in her head. She imagined a world where she could live as a normal human alongside someone with dark skin. Sure, she technically already did that now, but this time she could do it without feeling guilty. She could work with people who weren't Albino and not feel like she was betraying her own race. She could stand by their side and know that with everything going on, she wasn't turning a blind eye to the struggles of her people.

And that was just the Albinos. She wasn't considering what it would feel like for the Cybers.

"It's dangerous," Selena blurted quietly, realizing that it was literally the only defense that she had left.

"Yeah, no shit," Ivy chuckled. "But Selena, honey, are you trying to tell me that what we do right now isn't dangerous? The way we live now, using the undercity as a means of protection?" She scoffed.

"You've got to be kidding me if you think that's legit."

Selena hated to admit that her sister had a point.

She was about to object when the doors burst in. An Albino was being dragged in by his hair, screaming and kicking. The kid couldn't be bigger than 14 years old, and he was sobbing so loudly that the entire bar got quiet. The two Pure Skins who dragged him in were grinning ear to ear at what they had brought in, as if they were hunters smiling at their prized catch.

"Well, wel,l well," One of the men bellowed. He had a pot belly and was missing a tooth, and he seemed to have an almost cockney British accent. "Look what we have 'ere!"

Selena bristled. Ivy pulled her hood tighter.

"I'm sorry!" The Albino child cried. "I didn't mean to, I swear! I'll give it back!"

"Give us the bread back?" The second man, who was far leaner with a snake like tone, snarled. "You tainted it with your Albino skin! It's *worthless* now."

"Please," The boy begged. "I just wanted to have dinner! Please, my family is starving!"

"Well, just tell 'em that you're a lousy excuse for a thief when they're taking you to the free clinic for your medical bills!" The pot belly pig laughed.

Selena's upper lip curled in a rage. She started to stand up, but Ivy kicked her under the table.

Hard.

Selena glared down at her sister. "We have to do something!"

"No," Ivy hissed flatly. "We'll get spotted and arrested. We're not supposed to be here in the first place."

"No one will help him," Selena cried. "He's an Albino. They won't stand up for him and he'll get beat right here in the bar."

"It's probably not his first time, Selena."

Selena wilted as she realized with absolute certainty that she was right. Her sister was absolutely right. Selena could even see it with her own eyes as she looked at the young child. He was curled up in a ball, protecting his face in the way that only an experienced fighter would do.

Selena felt her heart shatter into a million pieces.

This was the kind of world that she could eradicate with the artifact that Ivy was talking about. This was the kind of life she could prevent young children from having if she joined the group. If she made sure, with absolute certainty, they would find it and put a stop to the abuse.

As the wails of the child filled the air, clouded by the cheering of the other Pure Skins, Selena decided right there.

She'd find that artifact if it killed her.

Chapter Two

When Selena was looking into the issues of her stolen material, she was beginning to wonder if she should use the artifact to simply remove all of the scumbags who liked to steal her stuff from the planet.

Sure, she had kept the screwdriver part that the rat had run away with. She was grateful that she had walked away with that one, but at the end of the day, she was still missing so many pieces of her original shipment. She had a feeling that the Hog and his men had something to do with it, but that wasn't going to change anything. She could have concrete evidence that the Hog and his men were the ones behind it and it still wouldn't change anything. She was screwed, and she knew it.

"What did they take?" Ivy asked, walking towards Selena's worktable, and putting her hand on her hip.

Selena's workshop was in the back of one of the bars that the Silver Blades ran - specifically, it was Ivy's bar. Obviously, the undercity was a dangerous place, meaning that most of the ways to generate income came from only the undercity kind of... economy. Pimping, soliciting from prostitutes, bars, drugs, you name it. Selena was lucky that Ivy was as powerful as she was. It was one of the only reasons that Selena was even able to make her name in the craft.

"They took at least three arm pieces and five leg bracers," Selena ran her hands through her hair. "It's not the biggest problem, don't get me wrong, but I have someone who is really in need of these products. If I don't get it to them, they will be stuck with some of the second-rate shit that I have stashed underneath these benches."

"I hate to admit it, Lena, but I think they're going to have to make do with the second-rate shit," Ivy sighed. "I don't think there's anything I can do for you."

Selena sighed. "I hate giving these to the veterans, Ivy. You know that."

"I know, honey," Ivy whispered in the fond way that only an older sister could. "But there isn't much I can do. Besides, you're already doing more for these people than they'd ever expect. None of them should give you a hard time about it."

She sighed and shook her head. Selena was about to argue that they deserved more because they had fought in the wars when the absolute last person that she expected to walk into her workshop stepped inside.

Ivy was the first to react. True to form when it came to the silver blades, Selena watched as a long dagger slipped into the palm of her sister's hand. Selena herself reached for her blaster gun taped underneath her workbench, but she wasn't as subtle as her sister.

The Hog simply smiled and raised his hands in surrender.

"I come in peace," His deep voice bounced off of the walls of the tiny workshop.

"I doubt that," Ivy snarled. Her voice reminded Selena of a snake.

Selena said nothing, instead keeping her lips pressed together in a firm line. She took in the Hog as she watched him. He was at least six feet tall, with a beer gut and a devilish smirk. He made his name not from how much he could kill you, but because he was the only Pure Skin in the game of the Undercity. He had money if you wanted it, meaning that if you pissed him off, there would be a bounty on your head in a moment's notice.

It was one of the only reasons Ivy didn't stab first and ask questions later - Selena knew her sister well enough to understand that.

"I have come to talk," He offered after a moment of awkward silence. "I promise. Trust me, I of all people are aware that starting a war with the Silver Blades is the dumbest move people can make in the Undercity. Evidently, a new faction here isn't."

Ivy lowered her blade, but only a little. Even Selena had to admit that the Hog sounded genuinely earnest. Ivy and Selena exchanged glances, neither sister really knowing what to say.

"Okay, fine," Ivy rolled her neck. "We'll listen."

"That didn't take as much convincing as I thought it would," He put his hands on his hips and raised his eyebrows. "I'm going to go on a hunch here and assume that you've had your run-ins with these so-called 'Pirate' sons of bitches as well?"

Selena immediately relaxed. Ivy, who was always prepared, simply just lowered her knife. She was still holding onto it, and Selena doubted that there would ever be a moment where her sister ever made a point to put it away when the Hog was in the room.

"Look, Selena," The Hog sighed. "I apologize in advance for any harm that may have befallen you, but I can promise you that it wasn't me or my men. We have a good business deal working here, I don't know why you think I would jeopardize it."

"I was thinking the same thing," Selena kept her voice flat and her expression dark. "It didn't seem to fit your M.O."

"That's what I said," he chuckled. "But regardless, someone *did* steal your stuff. Which, of course, I think is dirty. They don't know what you do here for these people, and they certainly don't know who you're protected by."

"Enough with the flattery," Ivy snapped. "Get to why you're really here."

"This is why I'm here," The Hog nodded. "I'm here to make sure I don't start a war with my only threat. And I'm also here to extend an alliance. Albeit a shaky one, since clearly none of you trust me." He chuckled. "It's not like I can't blame you. I wouldn't trust me either."

"Then give us a reason to trust you," Ivy countered.

Again, Selena said nothing. Ivy was always the one who took charge in business dealings like these. She was the one who always knew what to say and how to say it.

"Okay, so listen to me," The Hog offered. "The way I see it is that we have a common enemy. Quite simple, right? Easy to say. Now, imagine with me if you will, a world where we were united against these enemies. A world where we could be friends - or maybe just business partners -

until we figure out who the leader of this dumb clan is and squash them out for good."

Selena eyed her sister. It sounded like a decent idea, at least to her. She didn't know or understand these rules, though. She knew that, and she didn't pretend to know any different. She pretended instead to find that rearranging her toolbox was the best use of her time.

"I can admit that your offer is promising," Ivy crossed her arms. "But I still don't see what you get out of this. It seems to me that this is a one-sided deal, and you don't make those."

The Hog shifted uncomfortably and Ivy smirked.

"They took some of your drugs, didn't they?"

The Hog growled. "No, worse. My women. They make me more money than my drugs do on a good day. Whoever the leader of this organization is, they offered my girls more money in their pockets and freedom to decline clients."

Ivy scoffed. "Sounds like they have more freedom with this new guy - or maybe she's a woman."

"Maybe, but it's a shoddy business strategy," The Hog laughed. "If he's paying these women as if they're workers, he's never going to make enough money to make it in the Undercity."

"Then why does it matter to take him down?" Selena challenged.

She regretted speaking the moment that the words left her lips. She knew she wasn't someone who needed to speak up in business matters like the one that Ivy was handling, in the same way that she understood that not pissing off the Hog was probably the smartest decision she could ever make for herself.

And here she was, ignoring both of those rules. If she could have kicked herself in the face, she would have.

The Hog chuckled, but it didn't sound like a happy laugh at all. His eyes were dark as he took a few more steps, closer towards Selena. Ivy again raised her blade, but she made no move to use it.

"I mean, I understand where you're coming from, Selena. But you're not considering the big picture, are you?"

Selena blinked before looking at Ivy. She had no idea what he was talking about. What the hell was this 'big picture' that he was talking about? The women were getting paid, and they would probably leave for better pay.

"See, Selena, this is one of the reasons that I really like you," The Hog wagged his fingers. "You have a pure heart, and you don't expect the worst from people. You genuinely think that they're good people, and that everyone has a place in this world... Don't you?"

Selena crossed her arms. Sure, that was exactly what she believed, but the way that he was saying it... it just made Selena seem like someone who was a dumb and rather stupid child. She didn't appreciate that, especially since she was standing in her own lab of all places.

"What are you getting at?" Ivy demanded, crossing her arms.

"I'm just trying to explain to you two the concept of simple revolution," He laughed. "I wasn't sure if you knew about it, of course, but once you let the peasants start believing that they have a place in the world then they start to believe it. They start to want more - they start to hunger for more."

"Is that not a good thing?" Selena asked. "I thought the whole point of life was to work hard so you could accomplish your dreams."

The Hog burst out laughing in a dark, deep belly laugh. Essentially, it wasn't a funny laugh. It made Selena's blood curdle inside of her veins, and if she had the chance, she had a feeling that she would flee right then and there.

"You truly are a gem, Selena," He wiped a tear from his eye. "Never change."

Selena frowned.

"This is bold talk coming from you," Ivy leaned against the wall. "Not all of us are Pure Skinned like you. You talk about the peasants and forget that you're in the room with two of them."

The Hog again laughed, but this time it was a legitimate laugh. "You really believe that?"

Ivy and Selena exchanged glances before Selena said, "We have lived in a one-bedroom hut for the entirety of our lives. I think, yes, we do embody the lives of the peasants."

"Then you would be thinking completely wrong," He snickered. "Think about it this way - you were born into poverty, but are you *actually* suffering?"

Selena paused to think about what the Hog was offering. She hated comparing trauma because from one person to another it wasn't a fair comparison. But... Selena and Ivy had done well for themselves when it came to the hand in life that they were dealt. Selena was a successful underground scientist with a solid clientele who would do literally anything for her. Ivy had risen in the ranks of one of the most terrifying gangs in the undercity. It was obvious that they were major players when it came to the Undercity itself - they were literally having negotiations with the Hog.

Selena rubbed her arms uncomfortably, causing Ivy to sheath her blade. The Hog visibly relaxed.

"Maybe Selena could experience better since she can pass as a Pure Skin, but I can't. I had to claw my way to the top of where I am right now."

"Oh, trust me, I'm well aware," The Hog smiled. "I remember hearing the horror stories about the Silver Blades' latest recruit. I lost many a man to you for some years."

Ivy looked down at her hands and said nothing. Selena wondered then if Ivy was proud of what she did. She wondered if she enjoyed fighting those people, taking their lives so that she and Selena could eat.

At the end of the day, humanity was just another branch of the animal kingdom. We were all fighting to survive here.

Selena sighed. "Look, Hog, I don't understand what you're getting at here."

"Of course you don't," The Hog laughed. "You're a sweetheart. You'd never get it. Your sister, though... with the things she's seen, I'm sure she'll understand what I mean."

Ivy sighed through her teeth. It came out sounding like a whistle - it was one of her weirdest talents that Selena found herself jealous of from time to time.

"We have cushy positions here, Selena," Ivy explained. "If the working women started making something for themselves, it could threaten our way of life."

Selena gasped. She covered her mouth with her hands, mildly enraged. She knew that what her sister was saying was right, but she also knew that she hated it. And she had every right to hate it.

"I don't believe this," She whispered. "I can't believe this."

"I know," was all that Ivy could offer.

"So, you're essentially asking us to make life harder for everyone who works in the undercity by teaming up with you and stopping these Pirate people from giving working girls the opportunity to rise up?"

The Hog crossed his arms, and Selena wondered if she had crossed a line. Knowing herself, it wouldn't shock her if she did. She brushed some hair behind her ear and chuckled to herself, but the Hog didn't laugh.

"No," he said flatly. "That's not at all what I just said. You're making it seem like I'm some horrible person who doesn't want women to have dreams."

Selena narrowed her eyes. "That's only because it's true," she said. "At least, from what you just told me. Don't gaslight me and make it seem like you're the one who's innocent in all of this."

He rolled his eyes, but Selena stood her ground. He could tell her to stop making him out to be something that he wanted as long as he felt like talking to her - but the truth of the matter was still the same. She was simply calling him out for who he was.

"Fine. Maybe I don't want them to chase their dreams, but can you blame me? I mean, think about it, girls. We're criminals. There's no honor code between us. There must always be someone below us that we can step on to get where we are."

"Sounds like you're describing politicians, not street criminals," Ivy sneered.

"Yeah," Selena teased. "I thought having an honor code was what separated us from politicians."

The Hog pinched the bridge of his nose and sighed. He didn't look like a feared mob boss - in that moment, he looked like a father to several quite annoying teenage girls. Selena kind of enjoyed herself at that moment. It made this terrible person seem human, even if it was for a fraction of a second.

"I know that it sounds like I'm being mean, and I'll admit that I am," The Hog raised his hands in the air. "But think about it this way. Most of those working girls are addicts. Cybers, even. What happens when they get a lot of money to use on their own? Where do you think they're going to spend it on? They aren't Pure Skins. It's not like they can walk downtown and buy a place to stay. It's going right up their arms or into their upgrades forcing them to go further down into the system."

Ivy and Selena didn't say anything. They didn't want to admit that the Hog was right, in a way. It was the optimistic view conflicting with the pessimistic view. Selena could dream all day, every day, that these women were going to use the money to better themselves. She could imagine a world where that was the plan, but she also knew from experience and her life on the street that wasn't the case for many of these women.

Like the Hog said, there wasn't much else out there for Cybers and those who weren't Pure Skinned.

"Look, I'm not saying that I'm a saint," He admitted. "But I need you to understand that there's a lot more at stake than just preventing women from 'leveling up' in the world. There is no room to level up in this society. You two would know."

Selena nodded and pretended to start fixing something at her desk. She didn't trust her face not to show her plan with Ivy to find the relic. They hadn't talked about it since being at the bar, but Selena had thought up plans and all kinds of other ways to make finding the relic the easiest thing since sliced bread.

"Okay, so you want us to work with you and get these Pirates out of both our hair," Ivy nodded. "I'll run it by my boss, since I'm only second in command, but even I have to admit that I don't see her disliking this plan. I just want to know, what's in it for us after we take them down? Are we going to be best friends or will you double cross us?"

The Hog smiled. "Why would I double cross you?"

When Ivy tilted her head to the side and put her hand on her hip, the Hog let out a loud bellow.

"Fair," he chuckled. "I'll admit that much. Now, I can meet with your boss and discuss things -"

Ivy held up her hand and laughed back at him. "You're funny if you think that's going to work. You know damn good and well that the leader doesn't reveal themselves."

The Hog's face deflated, and Selena pursed her lips together to prevent herself from smiling. She knew the rules of the Silver Blades. Everyone knew the rules of the Silver Blades, including the Hog. The leader of the blades never revealed themselves for their own safety - if people found out, they would possibly be hunted down and attempted to be killed. It would certainly not be successful, but that was their party line for not revealing their leader's identity.

Selena had a feeling it was like that so the leader could assassinate their targets easier from the crowd. No one knows who to look out for. It was a terrifying thing to be wanted by the Silver Blades - no one had any idea where they would be hiding.

"Can't blame a man for trying, can you?" The Hog raised his arms.

"I can," Ivy narrowed her eyes, "But I won't. Just tell me what the plan is for after we stop the Pirates."

The Hog sighed. "My thought is that everything will go back to normal. It wasn't like we were enemies before this, anyway. We handle different things."

Selena's ears perked at that. She was pretty sure both gangs had their hands in everything - from drugs to sex trafficking. What were the Silver Blades not involved in, and why?

Ivy finally sighed and shook her head. "Look, you of all people know I can't make deals without talking to my boss. I will get back to you soon, though."

The Hog dipped his fedora and offered a really toothy and incredibly uncomfortable smile. His grin sent shivers down both girls' spines.

"I appreciate that, Hand of the Silver Blades," he smiled. "I expect to be hearing from you and your boss sooner than later."

Selena again said nothing. Ivy nodded in her stead, sheathing her blades as a sign of commonality. The Hog's grin grew wider in appreciation as he realized exactly what Ivy had just done.

"Well then," The Hog chuckled. "I will take this as my cue to leave."

As he was turning to leave, he passed a Cyber who was on their way into the clinic. He was limping, and he was covered in a cloak. Selena knew him, but she didn't dare call out his name. Instead, she just smiled at him.

"It appears you have a customer," The Hog chuckled.

"Don't keep them waiting long. Word travels fast down under."

And with that vague goodbye, the undercity leader vanished into the night.

Chapter Three

Selena's client, an old war vet named Kenneth, lowered his cloak and frowned.

"What the hell is he doing here?" Kenneth snarled.

Selena sighed. "He had some business to attend to here. Go ahead and take a seat, I'll get to looking at that leg."

"I don't like him," Kenneth continued talking as if Selena hadn't already dismissed it. "I don't like him here alone with you ladies."

Ivy smirked at him. "Are you assuming that I couldn't handle myself, Kenneth?"

Kenneth laughed. He had a deep and hearty laugh, one that was contagious for everyone around him. It was so contagious that even Selena found herself smirking.

"Fair point, Ivy. Fair point."

Selena grabbed the new part that almost cost her more than it was worth and wiped it off one more time. She didn't like that the rat had run off with it - they were unsanitary and she didn't want to put anything that touched a rat going into a human.

"I hope finding that part went alright," Kenneth offered.

"It was kind of messy," Selena admitted. "Some people tried to steal it from me. Actually, a rat stole it from me first."

Selena pulled back Kenneth's jean pant leg, rolling it all the way up to his knee. Then, she pressed the trigger releases on the sides of his fake patella bone and ejected the old - and rusted - calf piece. She put it back in the scrap box and grabbed the new piece.

"A rat ran away with it!?" Kenneth laughed.

"Yeah," Selena smiled but didn't offer much more.

Ivy's eyes brightened mischievously, looking almost like headlights as she smirked.

"Say Kenneth, have you heard anything in the undercity about a new gang called the Pirates?"

Kenneth's eyes widened. "A *new* gang? I thought all the spots were filled up."

"Well, you'd be right," Selena offered. She shook her head from side to side and sighed, then put her hands on her hips.

"You did not oil like I told you too."

Kenneth shrugged and tried to smile as Selena shook her head in disappointment. She went to grab more oil as Ivy sat on a stool next to Kenneth.

"So, listen, Kenneth," she smiled. "May I ask what you've been up to lately?"

"Nothing much," He sighed. "Just the usual, begging for money in the day and drinking in the evening. Just the kind of life I dreamed about when I was a soldier. Why does it matter to you what I did today?"

"Well, I'll take that as mild appreciation for asking about your day," Ivy snickered. "But listen, Kenneth, your old war buddies. What have y'all heard on the street?"

"Nothing crazy," Kenneth winced a little bit as Selena started to oil the metal in his legs - and in turn, his old human muscle. Even after all these years, it still hurts.

Selena did her best to make this part hurt less, but there was only so much that she could do.

"The Pirates are new," Ivy offered.

The thumping of the bass from the clubs outside made the building bounce. Ivy stood slowly and went to Selena's toolbox before hanging it on the hook that Selena had put up just for that.

"I was just wondering if they had tried to recruit anyone."

Kenneth let out a mild cry, and Selena flashed him a smile.

"All done," She promised. Then, she decided to take this as the perfect opportunity to scold him.

"If you oiled your leg every day like I told you to, your tune ups wouldn't hurt that much."

"I know," Kenneth let out a gasp of air before smiling. "I'm sorry, Selena."

"If you were really sorry, you'd start oiling your leg," She teased, but still smiled at him. She went to clean his cosmetics piece before tuning back into Ivy's questioning.

"I don't think that they've done any formal recruiting or anything," Kenneth sighed. "At least, not that I've heard. But you two know I'm an old geezer; there isn't anything that I can do for any gang at this point. You guys know this."

Ivy sighed and nodded. "I know... I just was hoping that maybe there was something else I could figure out."

Selena shot her sister a sympathetic smile before attaching the plastic piece to Kenneth's leg. Kenneth rolled his ankle around for a minute, then slowly got to his feet.

"Oh Selena, you truly are a saint," He smiled.

Selena smiled back. This was her favorite part of the job: seeing these people with nothing come to her for help, making sure that they understood that nothing that came from her cost anything. Kenneth already looked healthier as he wrapped Selena up in one of the tightest hugs she'd ever been a part of. She smiled and watched him hobble out at first, smirking as the hobble turned into a steady stride.

"You really are a magician with your gadgets," Ivy offered.

"I could say the same for you and your blades," Selena smiled. "But I know that face. You're thinking about something big. What is it?"

"Well..." Ivy rubbed the back of her neck. "Look, we need that team. The quicker we can get the relic the better that this world can become."

"You're putting a lot of faith in a mythical relic that we may not even know is real, you know."

"I'm just saying that even if it is, it's worth checking out. Don't you think so?"

"I know so," Selena nodded. "I just worry that we're putting too much faith in it. We know nothing about it."

"I know," Ivy sighed. "I'm sorry. I know it's a lot, but with these Pirates... I don't like what we're seeing. I know that they're capable of some pretty nasty stuff."

"How do you know what they're capable of? Aren't they new?" Selena tilted her head to the side.

Ivy sighed. "I don't know exactly what they're capable of yet, you're right. But Selena, think about the seriousness of what we've seen from them in simply one day. They challenged the Silver Blades, and they're stealing from The Hog. They're pissing everyone off."

"Doesn't that just mean they'll die quicker?" Selena offered.

Ivy shook her head. She looked paler than normal.

"I don't know, Selena," She admitted. "These attacks... They seem coordinated. Something that a regular person wouldn't know how to do, let alone understand. I feel bad saying that, but it's true. I just... ugh."

"I get it," Selena smiled. "I know it's hard, but there's a lot going on right now. Besides, how do we even know that the Hog was telling the truth? He could be totally wrong."

"If he was wrong, why do you think he would come to *us* for advice?"

Selena paused. She hated to admit that it was a solid point from her sister. The Hog wasn't a man who was easily swayed, and he didn't easily trust, either. If he came to Ivy, the only one that he knew could contact the leader of the Silver Blades, then he must have been desperate.

"I...I don't know," Selena sighed. "You're right."

"I hate to break your heart, honey," Ivy whispered. "I know that you don't want to think about things like this, but you must. This is what my world looks like, and it's in danger."

"Then shouldn't we go after the Pirates instead of looking for a magical thingy-majig that could fix everything?" Selena cried.

Ivy shushed her by holding one finger to her lips, then smiled.

"But isn't looking for something magical more fun?"

Selena wanted to be angry, but she knew that she couldn't be angry. Her sister was right. The idea of hunting something magical from the world before was already more enticing than everything else.

"Okay, fine," Selena sighed. "I'm down. But before we start making any crazy plans or recruiting people, I need to make one more delivery. Is that okay?"

Ivy narrowed her eyes. For a second, Selena wondered if her sister would say no. She was older, but that didn't mean that she could boss Selena around. It also didn't mean that Selena would challenge her sister in arguments about going out at night. Ivy knew better than most what these streets held.

"Where are you going?" Ivy asked calmly.

"Marion's house," Selena answered truthfully. "I fixed Kenneth's leg but Marion is still bedridden. Apparently, the surgery went well and she's ready for her parts."

Ivy sighed and pinched her nose. "She sold the leg?"

Selena nodded and looked at the floor.

Selling healthy limbs was one of the most gruesome parts of the undercity, but it was also the most fruitful. The Pure Skins who lost limbs to cancer or battle and refused to have any Cybernetics in them demanded to have limbs. So, if some of the people in the undercity needed money, they would offer to get their perfectly healthy limbs chopped off. They would be compensated healthily, but they would also be doomed to a life as a Cyber forever. A lot of the undercity mob bosses understood this concept, and often... borrowed... unwilling participants to give their spare body parts. Then, they would sell them as their own.

In the undercity, it wasn't just your purse you had to watch.

They could take your legs.

Selena hated it, but she understood why people did it.

"Marion has five kids," Selena tried to explain. "Her husband died a month ago. She's doing what she has to do."

"Aren't we all," Ivy shook her head.

"I just want to help her," Selena offered, shaking her head.

"I know you do, sis," Ivy smiled. She walked over and kissed her sister's forehead. "I know you do. That's who you are."

Selena smiled sheepishly. She loved that her sister understood her like that, but on some days, she wished that Ivy was more like her. More loving and understanding of others. But even Selena had to admit...

It was Ivy's ferocity that kept them alive this long.

"I need to talk to the Silver Blades," Ivy nodded. "They need to know of this new... development. Go to Marion's and come straight back. Wear your cloak."

Selena nodded, knowing that she didn't even want to protest.

Her cloak was one of her most prized possessions, but it was also a way for Ivy or anyone else from the Silver Blades to track her down. She understood the importance of wearing a cloak with this pattern, too. Everyone in the undercity knew that she was part of one of the most vicious gangs in the world. They didn't know she was just a measly mechanic, of course, but that didn't matter.

No one was willing to gamble with the Silver Blades.

Ivy gave her sister an affectionate head pat before turning back on her heel and leaving the room. Selena then made her way towards the back and grabbed a satchel with her package in it. With her cloak on and her hood up, she made her way into the night.

Chapter Four

The night was never boring.

The moon rising into the sky only brought people in the Undercity out to play. Selena kept her eyes straight ahead, her satchel hidden, and her stride quick. She knew the rules of walking alone at night. Look busy, look dedicated, and look angry. Not that many stopped people who looked angry and busy, and they often did not try to mug those people either.

Out of the corner of her eyes, Selena could see prostitutes on the street catcalling the drunk men leaving the pubs, laughing and whistling at them. Cybers sat on the street corner, shaking their change cups, and begging for something to get them through the night.

In the shadows, Selena could see gangs waiting to rob and hurt. Her trained eye from the streets could immediately locate The Hogs' new hires, trying to prove themselves to the mob boss by preying on anyone walking the streets. In the darker shadows, almost blending in with them, would be where the Silver Blades were waiting.

Selena only knew where to look because of Ivy.

Naturally, no one was bugging her. No one even tried to stop her to talk. In fact, she was so close to Marion's that she could hear the giggles and cheers of children.

But then, she felt something near her shoulder.

She sidestepped immediately, hoping that it was nothing. But, like everything in the Undercity, of course it was something. A man in a black ski mask was reaching for her, but Selena was having none of it. She screamed, trying to reach for her blade on the hilt of her belt. But her scream was cut off by someone coming up behind her to cover her mouth.

How did she not hear them? Who were these people? Did they know who they were messing with?!

Selena bit down on the hand and smirked as the person who grabbed her screamed in pain and wagged his hand. Selena tried to take off running, putting some distance between her and her would be assailants. However, as soon as she took off running, she hit what felt like a wall.

Instead, it seemed to be someone's chest.

She stumbled backwards, then took this person in with a gasp. He was a tall man with dark eyes, but that was all she could see. He was covered in black garb from head to toe, so she couldn't deduce anything else from what she saw.

She opened her mouth to scream, but this man also covered her mouth.

With a cloth.

Selena immediately felt dizzy. She started to stagger, and her eyes were heavy.

"No..." she mumbled. "Stop... leave me... alone," she coughed.

She could feel her feet falling out from underneath her. She knew that within moments she was going to collapse. But...

She didn't.

Through her haze, she could feel the big man lowering himself with her. He held her, rather gently, until she was on the pavement. He gently lowered her head onto the ground before shouting orders to the other men, muffled from her exhaustion.

Selena had no idea who these people were, or what they were doing, but she knew they would be sorry. The Silver Blades would find her and rescue her.

She felt someone pick her up. She prepared to be tossed aside like a sack of warm potatoes but was pleasantly shocked to find herself held like a bride. The big man held her close to his chest, and she could hear him talking but couldn't decipher what he said.

She fell asleep to the sound of his heartbeat, rhythmic and calming, against her ear.

———-

When she woke up, she felt like she had the most annoying headache known to man.

She wasn't a drinker by any means, so she was never aware of what many people in her life complained about when they talked about hangovers. She never understood how something could cause your head to hurt that badly until she woke up feeling this splitting pain in her skull.

"Ugh," was the only sound she could make as she raised her hand to her temple, rubbing her head and groaning.

For a second, she had forgotten where she was. She didn't realize that she wasn't in the comfort of her warm, soft bed back home. She couldn't hear Ivy in the kitchen, humming as she made some kind of tea. The sun wasn't gently climbing in their windows.

No, Selena was somewhere else.

That's when she remembered the kidnapping.

She sat up fast on accident. It was so fast that her head was spinning from the pain of it all. She grabbed her skull and lunged forward, having to grab the floor and paw at it just to keep her standing up. She fought the urge to hurl all over the floor.

"I wouldn't do any sudden movements," A deep voice boomed from the darkness. "You won't like it."

Selena swallowed a scream. She didn't know who was talking to her and she didn't want to come off as a scared little kid...

Even if that was entirely 100% what she was.

She backed up as fast as she could against the wall, pressing her back to it and feeling her heartbeat race in her ears. The wall was cold cinder blocks, and she could feel the indentions press against her skin. She was still wearing what she wore the night before, thank God. None of her clothes had been removed, and the jacket she was wearing was still glued to her skin from the sweat.

Silence filled the room. It was almost a stuffy presence. Selena knew she couldn't smell silence, but she would be lying if she said that she couldn't smell the burning spice of the tension caused from the lack of words.

Finally, there was a bit of laughter. The deep voice had chuckled about something that was probably funny in retrospect, but something that Selena didn't personally find funny. He took a step forward, and she could hear what sounded like the clank of chains slapping against his clothes.

"Really? Nothing to say?"

Selena pressed her lips together, forcing herself not to say anything.

"Wow," The voice echoed. "I have to admit, I expected a bit more fight from the sister of the Silver Blades."

Again, Selena said nothing. She wasn't going to say anything to incriminate herself or even rile this guy up. She didn't know him, but clearly, he knew her. So, if he was an idiot who knew what he was getting into, then he should leave it at that.

"I wonder," He pretended to ponder. "If I called your sister right now and told her where you were, would she come running to find you?"

Selena shrugged, pulling her knees to her chest.

The voice made a disgruntled and agitated grunt. Selena could hear him get closer, and in the darkness, it was impossible to tell where he was hiding. Suddenly, there was a spark of a match.

For a second, as the blaze reached the climax, she could see a face. Then, as quickly as it appeared, it was gone.

"I can't see you," he sighed. "And you can't see me. So, let's shed some light on the subject, huh?"

The match hit what Selena could almost imagine was a stick of some sort judging from the sound. It was some kind of torch. As soon as the rag wrapped around it was engulfed in flames, Selina couldn't contain the gasp that came from her voice. She slapped a hand over her mouth in an attempt to keep herself quiet.

The man standing before her was *huge*.

He was at least six foot three. He was bulky and large in the sense of someone who had eaten nothing but protein since he was a child. His face was angular but handsome, with a long scar running down his cheek. His lips were pressed together in a thin line as he stared down at Selena before smiling.

"What?" he asked. "Did I scare you?"

Selena swallowed.

She would be lying if she said no.

His black, curly hair was falling into his eyes as he got down on one knee in order to get level with Selena's line of vision. She found that to be a rather kind gesture, considering, and was almost touched by it.

"No," she lied. Her voice came out as a tremble as he smirked at her.

"Liar," he snarled. "I can smell your fear."

Selena didn't doubt that for one moment.

"Is the only word you know the word 'no?'" he scoffed. "Seems like it's the only thing you feel like telling me, at least. How rude is that?"

Selena still couldn't say anything. Her mouth wasn't moving, and it wasn't entirely her fault. She wanted to say something, wanted to let him know that she was at least trying to talk and communicate but she couldn't.

She was too terrified.

"Listen," he whispered. "You have something I need. I can take it from you easily, or I can take it from you against your will. I know that you know where the rRelic is."

Selena blinked. She swallowed the fear as best as she could before narrowing her eyes at this stranger in front of her who obviously held her life in his hands. She rubbed her shoulders and tried to come up with something to say, but before she could his hand shot out from the shadows and grabbed her hair.

Hard.

She screamed like a stuck pig, fighting his attempts to move on her. She tried swatting his hands away, but he used his other hand to catch her other wrist.

"Don't," He snarled. "I don't think you understand exactly what kind of trouble you're in, dear. You know where the Relic is, and if you don't start opening your stupid little mouth, I can't help you."

Selena wanted to cry, but she couldn't. The tears physically wouldn't fall from her face. She imagined that the fear she felt in heart had grown so much that she might burst into tears. The stranger's hand on her hair was yanking, hard, against her scalp. The pain was a burning sensation - it reminded her of someone ripping duct tape off her leg.

Her lower lip quivered despite herself, and she watched the man from the shadow's face break out in a smile.

He tugged harder.

The yelp that escaped Selena felt inhuman. She'd never made that sound before, but then again, she'd also never had hair follicles yanked from the scalp. She batted her eyelashes a little bit, still not crying.

"I can rip pieces of your hair out one by one," he growled. "You know I can do that, right? I'm capable of it."

"I don't know where it is!" Selena suddenly screamed.

The man dropped her hair. Her head fell forward from the lack of tension holding her head up. She rocked forward, nearly falling face first. She swallowed and tentatively raised her free hand up to her pounding and burning scalp. Her other hand was still suspended in the captors grip, which tightened.

"Lies," he whispered.

"No, seriously," Selena begged. His grip on her wrist was getting tighter and tighter. "I don't know where the Relic is. My sister were thinking about looking for it. She just now even told me that she wanted to look into it."

"That's funny," The captor laughed darkly. "Because when we found your sister's messenger today; they were telling her that the shipment of pieces for the Relic was ready. Are you telling me you knew nothing about it?"

Selena was genuinely stunned. She was sure that her sister hadn't found anything - why did the messenger have something different?

"I don't take part in my sister's dealings," Selena answered honestly. "Really. I have no idea what she does on a regular basis, okay? I... I thought we had no idea where it was."

"So, she kept you out of the loop?" he asked. His breath was hushed, and it reminded Selena of someone trying to tell her a secret. "Really. You expect me to believe that."

"Please," Selena begged. "Really. I can't tell you anything else. I wish I could."

There was a pause. After a long moment, the man sighed and stood up. His large dark shadow covered the only light that seemed to be pouring into the room. From what she could tell, the man was large enough to reach the top of the room. Selena felt her heart skip a beat - from fear or something else, she wasn't sure.

"See, the thing is, Selena," he sighed, "I can't trust that you're telling me the truth."

Selena's body went cold. She wasn't sure what to do anymore. Her breath came in and out sharply in thin bursts. Her head was pounding where her hair was pulled, red hot and fast.

"So, either you can tell me a lie one more time, or you can wait until your sister's pitiful attempt to save you comes out and we capture *her* to get the truth."

"She won't do that," Selena lied through her teeth. "She won't say anything to you."

"Oh, but I think she will," the man laughed. "I think we have something that she wants more than you know."

"What would that be?" Selena snarled.

"You."

That was the last thing Selena heard before she watched the large man leave and slam the door behind him.

Chapter Five

Selena tried to count the minutes, but it was hard.

The seconds always built up on one another, and then she would run out of time. She tried making marks on the floor to no avail. So, instead, she found herself lying on her back and counting the seconds as they led into more and more minutes.

Eventually, she fell asleep.

She wasn't sure when the door opened. The only thing that she knew was that it was morning. There was more light coming through the cracks in the walls, and she could smell fresh rolls and cinnamon coming off of whoever came to get her.

"Rise and shine, little bitch," someone snarled. "It's time to *play.*"

Selina's mind began to race. She was a woman, and no fool. She was at their mercy. She knew what was coming for her, no matter what she tried. She closed her eyes for a bit longer, hoping it was a bad dream.

Then she felt the hands on her.

They were clawing at her, pulling at everything that she had on her. Nails dug into her skin. She screamed in anguish in an attempt to get them to leave her alone, somehow someway.

But she knew better than that.

She was in for something terrible, and she knew it.

They dragged her towards somewhere in the darkness. She wasn't entirely sure where they were taking her, but she knew in her soul that none of what was going to happen to her was a good thing. She shivered as they threw her forward onto a chair.

The chair that they threw her on was wood. She could tell from the way that the splinters underneath her bottom made her feel so uncomfortable, stabbing into her skin. She was just glad that they were allowing her to keep her clothes on.

The realization of what she just thought sent a chill down her spine.

"You have something we want," someone growled. This voice was different, not like the man who had come into her room earlier. "And we know that you know it!"

Suddenly, there was light. The room was illuminated by one lantern in the room, held up by from what Selena could see as only a long pole. From the light and the shadows of the room, she could count about four people total. Three of them were hovering around her, and the fourth one was leaning against the back wall with his arms crossed and staring at her. This was the same one that came into her room before. Now that there were better lighting options, she could see that he had dark, curly hair. She couldn't tell anything else from the lack of light, but she focused on that instead of the other three surrounding her.

"I told him I didn't know anything about the relic," Selena offered. She tried to keep her voice away from a whimper, not wanting to give any of them the satisfaction of her pain. "I really don't."

"You expect us to believe that you and your sister don't run in the same circles?" another voice snarled.

"No!" Selena cried. Then, she swallowed and tried to regain her strength. "No, we don't."

"I don't care if she doesn't know," A voice snarled from the back of pack of three. "I just want her to suffer."

Selena stilled. She knew that voice - it was from the man who she and Ivy had given the right comeuppance to after he tried to attack Selena.

"Yeah," he laughed. "Remember me, *princess?*"

Selena refused to look anywhere but at the unmoving man who was leaning against the wall.

He kept her gaze, unwavering.

Suddenly, the man she'd attacked in self-defense was the only thing in her view. His eyes were wide as he leaned closer, smelling like stale ale and urine of all things. There was a fresh, healing scar over his eye.

The eye, however, was the worst part of all of this. It was white and filled with blood in the iris. It made Selina squeamish, which she hated.

She squirmed and tried to look away from him as a reflex, and just as she imagined, they laughed at her.

If she was going to be squeamish from just an eyeball, she was in for more Hell than she thought.

"So, since I called dibs," the man laughed before grabbing something shiny from his belt.

A knife.

"You tell me where the Relic is, and I'll spare your eye."

Selena's breath hitched. She believed that he would do that - everything in her soul was screaming that there was nothing stopping him from getting his revenge from her.

"I don't know where it is," Selena begged. "Trust me, if I did, I would tell you."

They laughed. "An honest traitor, at least."

"Traitor?" Selena asked, trying her best to keep him talking.

"You're part of the Silver Blades, not the Pirates," He shrugged. "A traitor. Simple as that."

"But I'm not part of the Silver Blades," Selena promised. "I just run in their circles. My sister-"

"Sister this, sister that," the man sighed.

Suddenly, he jumped on Selena and held her face still with one of his big, meaty hands. The sweat from them rested of Selena's face, hanging to her skin with a ferocity. He held the knife right above Selina's eye, then moved it to her eyebrow.

Selena whimpered as the blade began to dig into her skin, drawing blood that ran down her nose and into her eyeball.

"Maybe if you scream loud enough, she'll hear you."

For a second, she tried to mentally be elsewhere. Literally anywhere else. Mentally, if she blocked out who and where she was, then maybe she wouldn't feel the pain coursing through her veins.

She couldn't believe how wrong she was.

When the knife dragged across her eyeball, the cold steel against her warm flesh is what shocked her the most. It felt sharper than the pain of the blade itself. The shock of that alone was probably the only reason that she didn't scream. Then it was hot. Red hot. Pulsing through her entire body. She began to shake and shiver in response to the feeling, but her lips didn't open to scream.

Nothing came out of her.

The man pulled the knife away from her eye, but she didn't even feel it or care. She blinked rapidly as a reflex, but each time she moved up and down with her eyelids it hurt. Sharp, hot. If she looked to the left, to the right, anywhere, she felt a sharp ache.

A mix of tears and blood fell from her face. She heard the man scream, but she couldn't see anything else.

Had he actually cut her eye out from her head? It only felt like he cut her, but she couldn't tell.

"You dumb WHORE! MAKE SOME NOISE, DAMNIT!" From her one good eye she could see the attacker raise his knife again.

For a horrifying moment, she wondered if he was going to actually take out what was left of her eye.

The man with dark hair grabbed the one eyed man's arm.

"Draon, stop," the dark-haired man snarled. "She's in shock."

"Then why isn't she screaming!?"

"Because she's in *shock*," The dark-haired man barked back. "You got your revenge. An eye for an eye."

"I didn't take her *eye*," the one-eyed man, or Draon, complained. "She can still see. I gave her a scar, to start. How else are we supposed to get information from her?"

"There are other ways," the dark-haired man argued. Something in his voice left no room for questioning or challenging him.

Draon lowered his arm. The dark-haired man walked closer to Selena, who's breathing was already becoming labored. Her good eye was open wide, and her body was slowly but surely registering the pain against her other eye.

She could feel the blood trickling down her eyelid. She hoped Draon was right, because right now she couldn't see at all.

The dark-haired man got on his knees so he could look directly at her.

"Oh, she'll talk," he grinned.

She could not *see*.

"I'm sure about that."

-—

Selena couldn't remember much else past the pain of her initial stabbing, cutting, whatever it was. She continued to fade in and out of reality. Whoever this dark-haired guy was, he knew what he was doing. He made sure not to just "keep going" with the torture, letting the pain and suffering sink in more before he jumped in and added any more.

Selena was terrified.

She could hear her own heartbeat in her ears. Her blood roared and her brain cried out for freedom. Where was her sister? Why was no one coming to save her? There was simply no way it was taking Ivy this long to find her, right?

Did Ivy leave her there to die? Were the Silver Blades unconcerned with Selena's safety after everything she had done for them?

She hadn't realized how long it had been when she heard the sound of something loud dropping on the ground in front of her.

On a reflex, her eyelids flew open.

She could see out of the bad eye - but it was blurry. She knew from her own experience and knowledge that the eyeball was one of the quickest healing organs, but she also knew that came at a price. She tried to close her one bad eye to prevent herself from making anything worse, but it was too hard.

Especially when she saw the black-haired guy standing there with a long, dark stick.

Was it a stick? She wasn't sure what it was.

"Selena," the black-haired man sing-songed. "Selena, wake up."

She struggled to lift her head up beyond just a little bit.

From where she was sitting, she could see that what was in hand wasn't a stick. Well, in a way it *was* a stick, but it was more like a stick with a string on it.

It took her a second to realize that the "string" she saw was part of a whip.

Her blood chilled.

The dark-haired man nodded, and suddenly hands were all on Selena. She wanted to scream and fight, but everything in her decided the best thing to do was save her energy. She needed to make sure that every ounce of her willpower, her desire to go on, was saved in a special little bottle that could eventually turn into her resolve. Fighting anyone wouldn't save her, and it would only make her life harder.

She let them toss her around, not paying attention to anything other than keeping one eye closed. Before she knew it, two of her hands were bound above her head and she was dangling by her feet. She could stand on a chair, thank God, otherwise her arms would have been ripped from the sockets. She doubted that her captors would have cared, but she did.

Her blouse was suddenly ripped completely off.

She paused, mentally. Selena didn't know what this meant - even though he was holding a whip, she was in a room surrounded by men in now only her bra. She heard some whistling and even some purring. Still, no one moved.

The dark-haired man circled her and walked behind her, the whip dragging slowly behind him on the stone floor. She didn't know what to say or do, so she remained silent.

"You can make this stop, Selena," his voice was soft.

She again said nothing.

He raised his hand and slowly touched her back. Sparks shot down her spine at the excitement and shock of his touch. His rough fingers danced over her delicate skin, tracing patterns, and touching her like a lover.

In a sense, it was almost cruel.

He sighed and took a step back, as if this experience was painful for *him*. He pulled his arm back - she could hear it from behind.

"Who is the leader of the Silver Blades?"

Selina said nothing.

The whip cracked loudly against the soft air, shattering the silence around her. She heard it before she felt it, hot and fresh against her back. A fresh mark - tearing the flesh of her back apart. Her mouth fell open in shock and nothing else as she blinked, slowly.

"Who is the leader of the Silver Blades?"

Selena said nothing, but this time she wasn't entirely sure that she could.

The second time, the shock and adrenaline had worn off entirely. She bit down on her lip so hard to prevent herself from screaming and giving her captors that satisfaction that she tore through the skin of her lip. Blood gushed through her own mouth as his body surged forward from the force of the whip.

"Boss," someone laughed. "She bit off her lip."

Selina knew she didn't, but she imagined it looked that way.

The pain of her lip wasn't even the strongest sensation that she was going through at the moment. She felt like a thousand bees were stinging her back multiple times over. The whip, she had known for a while, was one of the more painful methods of torture from the way that it was able to rip flesh from the most tender part of your body without causing any long-term damage - if you were lucky.

She was also well aware that people passed out from things like this. She was two whippings in and already gnawing off her own skin to keep herself from screaming.

The black-haired man stepped around to see the damage that she had caused to herself. He crossed his arms like a disappointed father and shook his head. He sighed, then ran his hands through his hair. The blood was coming in waves down Selena's chin. For a moment, she wondered if it was possible for her to actually have bitten through her lip. Maybe the adrenaline of it prevented her from realizing her strength until it was too late.

The black-haired man grabbed her chin and maneuvered her face from side to side, analyzing. He inhaled sharply, shaking his head.

"I think I've seen everything the human body does to cope with trauma, and then I'm proven wrong," he chuckled as if they had just shared a joke. Finally, he sighed.

"You can end this, Selena. I don't like doing this."

She looked up, gently, from where her head was hanging low. She smiled, blood dripping down her teeth, and said nothing.

The black-haired man seemed to get what she was saying. He sighed and took a step back, still holding onto the whip.

Through her bloody haze, she could see his eyes lower to her breasts. Her breathing caught for a split second, fear coursing through her veins, but he turned on his heel and walked back towards the whipping post.

"Who is the leader of the Silver Blades?"

Again, the whip came down. Selena startled herself by, again, not making a sound. This time, she wasn't sure why. The pain was so intense that it felt cold at first before it shifted to lightning jabs of utter pain and misery. Silent tears came from her eyes, dribbling down her face and onto her exposed chest.

"*Who* is the leader of the Silver Blades?"

The force of the next blow made Selina surge forward. Her body lunged toward the door, and she grunted. It wasn't a scream, but it was something. It helped, but only a little. She wished she could scream, but something in her subconscious didn't want to let the people in this room have the satisfaction of hearing that. They got to see it and that's all that they would get.

At least, if she could help it.

Blood tasted like copper. She found it a little strange - she knew it probably tasted like that. It wasn't a shock, but she didn't imagine it was real. She had heard Ivy describe it that way, and she had to admit that she wasn't entirely sure if she believed them until now.

She was swimming in blood. In an attempt to distract herself, she tried to analyze everything she learned about blood. The whip was hitting her back now, and she couldn't even hear the black-haired man anymore. She was dissociating to survive, and she was okay with it.

The sting was still there, but she could almost pretend that it was just a bug gnawing on her back. She imagined seeing a stream of blood in front of her. First, she thought about the color - maroon, soft red, dark. If it wasn't oxidized, blue. There were so many different ways to see and analyze blood. It tasted like rusted copper, like old pennies. She couldn't think of anything else to equate the taste of blood too - the salt was there, but it wasn't overpowering.

Suddenly, her eyelids became heavy. The cracking of the whip was alarmingly fast now, sounding more like firecrackers than anything else. She could feel the sharpness of the whip on her arms, legs, everywhere.

He was losing control, and she was losing consciousness.

It didn't seem in black haired guy's nature to lose his cool - she had to admit that she was a little impressed with herself for making him slip. As her body shut down and crumpled into itself, she smirked.

She won, even if it was a small win.

Chapter Six

When Selena woke up again, she was sore and sticky.

She hated the way that sounded in her head, but there was no other way to describe it. Her limbs were pulsing and sore, and the blood had clung to her skin to form an almost glue-like substance keeping her to the floor.

Her back was a wreck. She could smell the blood before she could truly assess the feeling of needles digging into the soft flesh of her back. She slowly rose from the stone floor, where hay was scattered for a makeshift bed, and pressed her lips together to keep from screaming.

Her torturer had *truly* lost control. When she was brave enough to touch her own back, she could feel nothing other than blood and strips of remaining flesh.

"At least I'll finally get a badass scar," she whispered to herself before forcing a smile.

Humor was a defense mechanism for a reason.

Her bottom lip was throbbing. She reached her hand to her mouth, already stained with blood from her touching her back, and tenderly brushed up against her bite mark.

She *had* torn through her lip.

Not hard enough to lose the entire bottom lip, thank God, but there was certainly a whelp of flesh and skin missing from her bottom lip.

Where the hell was Ivy?!

That was the thought coursing through her mind at the time. Her sister, the one that was supposed to protect her from everything, hadn't found her yet. Was she scrambling around on the surface, looking for her? Looking for clues? The fear that was swimming through Selena's mind was the question of whether or not her sister was taking the Pirates seriously. She remembered the conversations they had about the new gang, and she could only hope and pray that her sister considered them a valid threat.

That, or she would spend the rest of her days trapped down here. She had absolutely *no* idea who the leader of the Silver Blades was, which made not giving up any information about them that much easier. Part of her wondered if she would have given it up if it hadn't been for the fact that she didn't know, if if she would have been strong enough to not do that.

She guessed she would never know.

The door slowly creaked open. She winced, wishing she had spent the down time she had more productively. She wasn't mentally ready for whatever round 4 brought for her. Despite her fear, though, all she seemed to hear were shushings and demandings that everyone around them be quiet. She raised her eyebrow in concern.

Why did they have to be quiet?

"There she is," someone growled.

She could remember their voice from the whipping but couldn't place where. She could see multiple shadows flood the room but couldn't really do too much about it. She could barely sit up, let alone do anything else.

"Nick doesn't know we're here," someone else hissed. "We need to keep her quiet."

Nick? Maybe that was the name of the black-haired guy?

The reality of what was happening set in a bit too late. They weren't allowed to talk about it, Draon didn't know they were here, and they had to keep her quiet...

She was about to be raped.

The word felt fuzzy on her tongue. She tensed as hands found her in the darkness, but this time they weren't dragging anywhere. They were pinning her down.

She didn't mean to scream - she had fully planned on fighting until they killed her in silence - but when her bare back slammed against the stones, she finally released the scream that had been building inside her the entire whipping. It was loud, piercing.

"Shit!" one man cried. "Shit, I told you to keep her quiet Draon!"

Ah yes, the one-eyed man. Selena hated to say that she wasn't entirely surprised to hear that he was here.

She would take great pleasure in biting his dick off.

More hands held her down. She could feel at least one set of arms for each of her limbs - four men, at least. There was no way to physically fight them off. Selena was barely strong enough to carry her cybernetic pieces places, let alone fight off four men with one hand.

She was more shit out of luck than she thought.

She could feel two grossly large hands force her legs apart. She could hear the sound of unbuckling pants. The weight of someone heavy on top of her, holding her down. The pressure took all the breath out of her. Her back burned. Her mind raced.

She thought back to her first time, trying to imagine something else like she did when the whipping became way too intense for her to handle. She remembered the hands, gentle and kind, of her first lover. Of the way that he listened to her every want, to her every move.

Rough lips were suddenly on top of her mouth. She tried to move her head out of the way, but it was all she could do to keep her lips shut. One hand was unbuttoning her pants, and the other was holding her face in place. His tongue was trying to open her mouth, to get her to open it for him.

Then she got an idea.

She opened her mouth and relaxed, trying to throw him off as if she was super into it... then bit the ever-loving shit out of his bottom lip.

This time she made sure to keep her jaw shut, her teeth sticking heavily into the flesh.

She could hear him scream, and when he yanked his head back, she was still holding onto the lip. He was squirming, crying, wailing like a child. When he looked back at Selina, glaring, she smirked.

She spit his lip back at him, watching the blood splash over him.

"You BITCH!" Draon cried.

He used both his hands to grab her throat and squeezed. She couldn't do anything about that - the other men were still holding her down. She didn't want to die, but if it was to die or be their plaything, she would gladly slip into the other world.

"YOU STUPID WHORE! I'LL FUCK YOU WHEN YOU'RE DEAD!"

"Draon!" the man in the corner begged. "You can't scream like that! Nick-"

"Screw Nick!" Dragon yelled. "He can't do shit!"

The room was growing dark again. Selena's lungs fought for air as she squirmed - her body's last ditch effort to stop from dying. When nothing changed, her lungs gulped one more time for air. It felt like she was swallowing a lit match.

And then it was over.

She wondered if she had finally died, but her body kicked in before her mind did. She was gasping loudly for air and coughing hard. Why did Draon stop? Was he playing with her?

That's when she saw that the dark-haired man, Nick, was holding Draon up over her body by his throat.

Nick looked... different.

His eyes were glowing. She could see his sneer from the ground where she was lying down. She gasped and scrambled backwards, finally free from everyone else's grip. She almost didn't feel the stones dragging on her back.

"Looks like someone needs a reminder of who's in charge," Nick snarled in the deepest voice Selena had ever heard.

"I *said* that no one touches her."

Chapter Seven

Selena watched in shock as Nick continued to squeeze the neck of Draon. Selena could see the color draining from his skin, being replaced with a kind of blueish purplish tint. His hands were clawing ferociously at the grip that Nick had on him, trying to tear him away with a ferocity that Selina had never seen before. She blinked in shock before Nick threw Draon hard and fast at the wall.

He hit the stone wall with a loud, bone-cracking thud. For a second, Selena feared that the man had died after all. She was shocked at the fact that the first thought in her head was that he died too quickly - it made her wonder if there was something a little wrong with her when she considered it.

But she still thought it nonetheless, and with a smile on her face.

She watched in horror and fascination as Nick made his way through the crowd of would-be-rapists like a parted sea. No one even tried to stop him - it was almost like they understood their fate all too well and knew better than to try and stop it. Nick slammed heads against the wall, splitting skulls with a satisfying crash. Bits of brain flew out onto the floor, making a squishing sound as they collapsed.

After Nick slammed one head, the others decided that their best choice of survival was to flee. There was clearly no winning here, after all.

None of them got away.

Nick grabbed one of them by the hair and yanked down, hard. They collapsed from the weight of him and screamed for a split second before the boot found their face and crushed it underneath his heel like a bug.

One by one, the men fell. Finally, only Draon was left..

Selena had gathered herself and scooted back into a nearby corner. Her main goal was to try to stay out of his way and make sure that no one saw her and drew any attention to her. She could hear a few of the other men crowding the door, looking in with horror-stricken eyes. She could hear one of them vomit at the sight of corpses and fallen bodies. She couldn't help but smile at the scene before her.

Draon was still coughing. Selena couldn't tell if the man even knew what to do with himself at this point. The way he was staggering was enough to make him look a little drunk. Which was fair, considering the lack of oxygen that went to his brain when Nick had him in his grasp.

Nick slowly went to Draon. He grabbed him by his hair and dragged him to the middle of the floor where Selena was before. He whistled, and four men from the room stepped forward as they were commanded. Selina was impressed.

"Hold him down."

The men obeyed without question. Nick stood up while Draon struggled, begging and pleading for Nick to "have a heart." Nick ignored him, spinning the knife between his fingers as if it was a pen.

"I want you men to see this," he said. "I want you to see what happens when you ignore a direct order from your Commander. Not only will I kill everyone who tried to ignore my orders, but I will punish you as I see fit. See, men, Draon is a rapist."

Gasps filled the room. Clearly, the men didn't side with that kind of behavior. Selena found it comforting.

"Or at least, he tried. Our prisoner put up such a fight that he didn't get the chance."

She could hear some whistles, some "wows." She blushed, mildly embarrassed, and slightly confused with the change of events.

"Given the situation, I have an idea as to what to do to him before we kill him."

"No, please!" he begged. "Don't kill me. I promise I won't do anything. I won't. I'll leave you'll never see me again."

Nick spun on his heel and pointed his knife at Draon. "See, that's why I know you're lying, because I think it's pretty obvious that you're a vindictive man. I can't let you go; you know that."

He paled.

"What did they used to do to rapists in Rome, Kenny?"

One of the men holding down Draon immediately responded. "Crushed their testicles, sir."

"Yes, but see, since he was attempting, let's let him keep his balls," Nick lowered down to a squat and smiled at Draon.

He looked a little happy, exhaling. "Thank you, Nick. God, thank you."

Nick's smile melted almost immediately into a stone-faced expression of rage.

"Let's cut off his dick."

All of the color drained from Draon's face, but Selena smiled. Somewhere deep in her soul, she found herself feeling excited about this. She found herself anticipating their entire reaction. Part of her wondered if she was a bad person for thinking this. If she was a good person, she would have got up and told them that just because he was a terrible person who did a terrible thing to her didn't mean that he deserved the same treatment.

But her legs never moved to do that. Her smile was glued to her face continuously as she smirked, devilishly, directly at him.

She knew what was coming. She wanted it. He tried to take something sacred from her. Sure, it wasn't her virginity, but it was *her*. He tried to break her spirit and her soul, and when he couldn't do that, he tried to break her until she was no longer breathing.

She won. Even by luck, she figured it was only fair that he had the same thing happen to him. The only difference between the two of their chances of survival was the fact that Selena had a big, strong, and scary man come save her from his clutches. If he had been a terrible man, the roles very well could have been reversed.

But, as it turned out, he wasn't a terrible man.

She was lucky. When she gambled with her life, it seemed the gods smiled down happily on her. Sure, part of her wondered why, but she wasn't one to look a gift horse in the mouth.

"Please!" He screamed. "Nick, Nick! You're a man. Please, you know what this feels like. Nick. Nick, you have to understand! NICK!"

Selena smiled down at the scene in front of her.

Nick made two long incisions along the divots of Draon's pants, following the seams and where they went. She watched as he tore the fabric in two, smiled as her would be rapist thrashed and screamed. The four men holding him down were even having some trouble trying to keep him in place. He was crying like a baby.

Selena didn't want to judge him, but she was just in his position.

She didn't shed a single tear.

She scoffed. "Weak."

She watched some more as Nick tore away at the piss-colored underwear glued to his skin. What was exposed was the small, worm-like creature that was almost inside her against her will. She doubted she would have felt it.

It was shriveling backward, trying to hide back within itself. But Nick wasn't having it. Nick pinched the end and pulled it out, elongating it.

Draon screamed in shock before the blade came down.

It sounded like someone was chopping sausage, to be honest. There was nothing that made it sound different or crazy to someone on the outside.

But then came the wails.

Oh, the wails. They were piercing, heartbreaking. He was cursing in languages that Selena had never heard. He was sobbing, snorting, vomiting all at once. She was surprised he didn't pass out from the pain. She was sure that he would soon, so she enjoyed the moment of his suffering.

He was tossing, turning. Blue, pale. Everything she imagined that came with it was there, right in front of her. She couldn't help but smile.

And then it was over.

Draon fainted in a puddle of his own vomit. The blood from his useless dick leaked into the cobblestones. Nick's upper lip curled as he looked down at what used to be the man's dick before sheathing his bloody knife and standing up.

"I want him hung here by the arms. When he wakes, we hang him."

The four men that were holding him down nodded before going to do just that. Nick turned on his heel, then, turning his attention to a shocked Selena.

He moved to her with the force of a thousand suns. She panicked for a second, unsure what to do. Had he saved her from being raped just to take her himself?

He grabbed her forcefully, but she didn't struggle. He threw her over his shoulder with a thud, losing the air from her stomach as she winced. She wondered why he didn't carry her bridal style until she remembered her back.

Small mercies.

She couldn't see where they were going, but she wasn't sure she really wanted to consider. She remained still, knowing better than to make a fuss after what she just saw. Before she knew it, the hard steps on the cobblestone turned into steps on soft... carpet?

He gently removed her from his shoulder and laid her out on a large, cashmere bed. He put her facedown, and part of her prepared for him to rape her from behind. Why else would he bring her in here? He was the one who had her tortured, after all.

But no. Instead, he immediately backed off and sighed.

"I'll have a nurse come in here to dress your wounds. Sleep."

And with that, the door slammed behind her.

She blinked, confused. What the hell just happened? What was she feeling? Why did Nick save her?

What the hell was she in for?

—-

Shocking even to her, she slept hard.

After the trauma she went through, she had a bad feeling that she wouldn't be able to sleep ever again. She hated to admit it to herself, but the feeling of Draon's hands over her and lips on her body still made her shudder.

The only thing that gave her some peace of mind was the fact that she fought back, and that she fought back hard. It was this thought that allowed her to finally get some sleep. When she woke up, her body ached in a way that she couldn't even fathom. At first, she prayed that everything she had endured was just a bad dream. She prayed hard, but as she slowly came to her senses, she began to realize that the cold floor beneath her was a reality. It was real, no matter how much she wanted it not to be.

Slowly, her eyes peeled back. She could see some sunlight climbing into the room with her as she sat up, rubbing her head. Her back was the first thing that caught her attention. It throbbed with every movement she made, and the blood on the cobblestone beneath her was wet. She could tell because her shirt was soaked.

Wait.

Shirt!?

She looked down slowly, so as to not hurt her throbbing skull. She was wearing a huge white shirt, which probably belonged to the handsome savior from the night before.

The same one that whipped her like a dog, too, of course.

Not to be mistaken.

"Okay," She whispered. "Weird."

Shuffling in the room over made Selena jump. She gasped despite herself before she noticed a woman with an apron and a soft smile walk in. She had a cybernetic leg that creaked with each step.

"Oh, my dear, you're up!" Her soft voice bounced off the walls. "I wished I had heard... How long have you been up?"

"Not too long," she lied, but not so much. She had truly just woken up. "Thank you for asking."

"Master Nick made sure that I treated your wounds," She explained as she set a bowl of what looked like water and a rag down by her... bed?

Selena hadn't even realized she had been laying on a bed. Really, it was more like a cot, but it still wasn't the floor. With the cuts and tears on her back, the bed felt like cobblestone.

What the hell was going on?

"You've been out for three days," the woman wrung the towel out over the bowl. "You had a fever, thrashing a bit. Your back was borderline infected if it hadn't been for me."

Now that Selena was waking up, she could feel padding against the soft and threatened skin of her back. It had been treated.

But why?

"You... treated my wounds?" Selena whispered. "Why?"

"Nick told me to," the woman answered plainly.

She either wasn't getting what Selena was saying, or she didn't want to answer her.

"Why did he tell you to?" Selena asked. "I thought he hated me."

"Oh, he doesn't hate you," The woman chuckled. "I think he's quite fond of you."

Selena blinked in confusion. She wasn't sure how to process that.

How could he be fond of her and do what he did to her?

"I know it may not seem like it," The woman chuckled. "But I can't tell you that Nick is a good man. He takes care of us."

Selena laughed under her breath, shaking her head. "Sure. He may take care of you, but clearly, I was nothing but fodder to him."

The nurse shrugged. "If you were just fodder to him, he wouldn't have saved you from the rapists."

Selena winced. Her back ached, but not from the pain. It was more the memory of the pain that struck her. The memory of the hands on her.

"You heard that, huh?" Selena whispered.

"Don't be ashamed," the nurse wrung out a towel and walked closer to Selena. "Draon was a jackass, and I'm glad that Nick took care of him. I know that he did... well, this to you." The nurse gently lifted Selina's shirt and gestured to her back. "But you don't understand why we need to speak to the Silver Blades. It's a matter of the utmost urgency."

Selina winced and inhaled sharply through her teeth as the hot towel gently cleaned her scabs and scars. "Well then, why didn't you kidnap an assassin? I don't understand why you thought that I could get you anywhere with this."

"Because we know your sister is connected," the nurse continued cleaning. "We don't know how, but we've been warned about her. We understand that she's a force to be reckoned with."

"And yet you thought the best course of action in all of this was kidnapping the only family she had left?"

The nurse laughed. "Trust me, I wasn't the one who came up with *that* plan."

Selena heard her move some more. She knew that the leg was painful - she could hear the metal whining with each step the poor woman took. Selina suddenly felt something cold and sharp on her back and gasped - fear of being attacked or whipped again flowing through her veins like blood. But then... relief.

Sweet, sweet relief.

"Sorry, honey," the nurse whispered. "Lidocaine hurts at first but it's the best numbing agent we've got."

Selina didn't even hear her. She was too busy sighing in relief.

The nurse laughed and finished, lowering Selena's shirt. She put the rest of her equipment back on the table before turning to leave, but Selena had other ideas. She hated to admit it, but it was true. Despite what everyone in this cursed place had done to her, she still cared.

After all, like the nurse said, none of this was her idea.

"Wait," Selena asked. "Let me look at your leg."

The nurse blushed. "No, please. It's really nothing, I just need some oil-"

"You helped me," Selena whispered. "Let me help you. I'm a prosthetic mechanic. Please."

The nurse's eyes widened. "You're a mechanic?!"

Selena smiled. "Yes. Now can I see?"

The nurse ecstatically sat down on the bed, bringing her rusty leg up. She wasn't kidding about needing some oil, that was for sure. She inspected it and wished in that moment that she had her tools.

"Needs some oil, and I see a busted screw. If you could get me some machine oil, a rag, and a Philips screwdriver, I could fix it."

The nurse jumped up and limped as fast as she could towards a table that seemed to hold most of that. She handed the tools to Selena with shaking hands, and Selina did exactly what she did best.

Selena fixed the leg.

She didn't know what doing the mechanics of this was truly for-herself or the nurse. Being back in the realm of cogs and springs and machine oil was more than perfect for her mental health. With each squeak and cleaning being done, she could feel herself forgetting the whip and the would-be rapists.

Not for long, of course, but she wasn't about to look a gift horse in the mouth.

She almost didn't even hear Nick come in.

"I didn't know you were a mechanic."

His voice was low, grumbling. He startled both of them so much that they both gasped. The nurse was more of a playful shock, but fear stabbed Selena in the heart. She didn't mess up the leg that she was working on, though. Her hands were steady like always.

Nick raised his hands in defense as he leaned against the door. "I'm not here to hurt you, Selena. I feel that I've done enough of that."

Selena wanted to snap back at him. She wanted to shout at him and laugh at his snide remarks. No shit, he hurt her more than enough.

But he also saved her.

While her mind was swimming with the thoughts of what she wanted to say, her body didn't react. Her lips pressed into a thin line as Nick remained where he was standing.

"I took pleasure in killing Draon," He stated flatly as he looked down at his nails. He inspected them like a woman looking at her most recent manicure. "I did not take pleasure in hurting you."

"Somehow I doubt that," Selena whispered.

Nick sighed. "I know. You're allowed to be angry, Selena, but you need to understand that it's not like I'm some crazy mad man. I did *what* I did for a reason. I thought you were holding out on us."

"And I told you I wasn't," I whispered. "I swore to you that I wasn't."

"Right," He nodded. "But we don't know you. The same way you don't know us. You telling me the truth shocked me in the same way that me saving you from Draon and the others probably shocked you as well, did it not?"

Selena rubbed her arms and nodded.

"So, essentially, there's a lot we still need to learn about one another," Nick moved a little bit closer towards Selena. When she flinched, he again raised his hands in surrender but made no move to move forward.

"You fixed Barbra's leg."

The nurse who was sitting next to Selena nodded. "Yeah, she did!"

"No payment expected, obviously?"

"Of course," Selena nodded back. Part of her was slightly offended by the notion of even asking that.

"See, you are a good person, Selena," Nick explained. "I think you might be a bit sympathetic to our plight if you would just listen to us."

Selena looked to the side and swallowed. "Even if I listen," she whispered, "I may not be able to help you in the way that you think I can.

Everything you were asking me... I wasn't lying. I really truly didn't know what you were asking about."

Nick nodded. "Yeah, we kind of gathered that." Then, he sighed.

"We also know that Ivy, your sister, does know what we need. And I think, personally, that she's not going to let us take her sister slide. She'll be here soon, I'm sure. I'm surprised she hasn't come already if I'm being honest."

Selena smirked. "Fair."

"While we wait for her, I'm going to see if I can convince you to side with us. We could use the Silver Blades' help."

Selena laughed. It was a sound that, honest to God, she never thought she would make again. When Nick didn't seem to react to her laugh, she just simply shook her head.

"I would love to see how you convince me to side *with* you after everything you did to me."

Nick smirked. "Maybe once I tell you what we're after, you'll understand."

"Okay," Selena offered. "Try me."

Again, Nick smirked.

"We're after the Artifact of the Before, so we can topple the cult leaders and restore this country to what it was before. We're working for the people, Selena. People like *you*."

Epilogue

Ivy never knew Selena to be late, let alone go missing.

She didn't just run away, and she wasn't an Albino like herself. No one would nab someone as protected as Selena without knowing of the consequences. Not only could she blend in with the upper-class circles, but she was also a skilled mechanic. A loved mechanic that left many people in pain in her absence.

Selena hadn't been home in days.

Ivy's sisters of the blade had tracked her down to a warehouse hours away. When she realized the sisters took longer than a week to find them, she made sure that they regretted it.

She started with peeling back their fingernails.

From what she was able to discern, from the politics of the land none of the crime lords and assassins who were already established would have threatened someone connected so closely to the Silver Blades.

This had to the be the new gang, the Pirates.

Ivy would enjoy watching them all burn to the ground if they even laid a finger on her sister.

After all, the leader of the Silver Blades always got her way.

Don't miss out!

Visit the website below and you can sign up to receive emails whenever JM Steiner publishes a new book. There's no charge and no obligation.

https://books2read.com/r/B-A-ADNEB-ZUSYC

BOOKS 2 READ

Connecting independent readers to independent writers.

Also by JM Steiner

Cogs and Daggers
Cogs and Daggers: The Adventures of Ivy and Selena Book 1

LPS PUBLISHING HOUSE LLC

About the Publisher

LPS Publishing House LLC is commited to bringin quality books to its readers. Starting to branch out int fiction writing and covering a multitude of genres. There will be books for every type of reader. First starting out with their main author Magnus Carter we have signed a lot of very talented authors, creative writers, graphic designers, and the list goes on. You can find out more at our website www.lpspublishing.com

www.ingramcontent.com/pod-product-compliance
Lightning Source LLC
Chambersburg PA
CBHW022050170626
46808CB00003B/1426